THE MUD
PEOPLE

THE MUD PEOPLE

A Parable of Recovery

LANEY MACKENNA MARK

WARNER BOOKS

A Time Warner Company

Warner Books, Inc., 1271 Avenue of the Americas, New York, NY 10020
Visit our Web site at http://warnerbooks.com

 A Time Warner Company

Printed in the United States of America
First Printing: March 1998
10 9 8 7 6 5 4 3 2 1

Library of Congress Cataloging-in-Publication Data

Mark, Laney Mackenna.
    The mud people / Laney Mackenna Mark.
        p. cm.
    ISBN 0-446-52114-0
    I. Title.
    PS3563.A66254M8   1998
    813'.54—dc21   97-6253
                                             CIP

Book design and composition by L&G McRee

*Dedicated to my mom, dad, and sister Reeny,
whose mud was removed in death.
I love and miss you.*

*Dedicated also to Dr. David W. Phillips, who is a Juta to me
in real life. His wisdom, care, and gift of himself have
helped me greatly in taking my journey toward healing
and being mud free.*

Author's Note

*I*f you have experienced abuse or harm in any way, know that I have written this story for you. *The Mud People* is my story as it is that of many others, but my desire in writing it has been for you who are unable for any reason to give a voice to your hurt inner child.

For those who have died as a result of violence or abuse, I give the world your unheard voice. It will be silenced no longer. Your presence here on this physical plane counted, and you are missed.

If you are looking for your personal power by robbing it from others, I wrote this for you, also. It's not a story about blame or fault but about discovering where your power lies, which is within you. I pray this story touches you in a deep way, and that you will begin your journey to find where your real power is and therefore stop robbing it from others, especially children.

Blessings,
LANEY MACKENNA MARK

THE MUD
PEOPLE

CHAPTER 1

The Mud People

Not so very long ago there lived a little girl named Kaila, which means "filled with fright." She belonged to a family known as the mud people. Kaila and her entire family were covered with layers and layers of dirt and dried mud. They lived among the trees of a dark forest where the sun never shone, the ground was always damp, and the air misty. Because the sun never penetrated the dark forest, there were very few flowers that grew there, and those that did manage to survive were dull in color and almost lifeless.

Near the forest where Kaila's family lived flowed a beautiful river. Although the river ran right next to the forest, none of the mud people had ever seen it. This river was different from any other because it was said to have magical powers. On bright sunny days, the water took on the appearance of hundreds and hundreds of shimmering stars. There were even sightings of angelic beings floating in and around the river. Yes, it seemed to have a mysterious pull to it and could easily attract anyone brave enough to get close by. It was almost as if this graceful flowing water had a purpose and life all its own: to find the broken-hearted, lost, abused, and unwanted people.

Among the shadows of the forest there was much for a young girl like Kaila to fear. Very often members of her mud family were cruel to her. She was almost always criticized for her actions, laughed at for her fears, and put to shame. Kaila's thoughts as a young child about safety, trust, love, and closeness were just that, thoughts. They were not a part of her day-to-day life. As a matter of fact, she was warned by her mud mother *not* to think or feel! She told Kaila, "Such thoughts will only cause you great trouble and pain." Kaila's only way to understand the world around her was through the cloudy perceptions of her mud family.

However, despite the terrible cruelty and abuse shown Kaila by some of her mud family, she loved them. Not only did she love them, she felt compassion for them and longed to be close to them. She often wondered what *they* thought about and felt. She knew, of course, that like her they were well schooled in the family rules: no thinking or feeling. So, sadly enough, Kaila felt very disconnected from her family and spent her days in isolation and loneliness.

Kaila had an "inner friend" who often whispered to her, "There is more to life than what you've experienced here in the shadows of the forest." It also spoke to Kaila about a river that flowed by the forest just beyond the dark shadows of the trees. Kaila thought about this river and at times felt an urge to go to the edge of the forest and see what was there. Kaila wondered who this "inner friend" was and where it came from. Was it a part of her?

One day Kaila felt curious enough to wander near the river. There, on the riverbank, grew tall grasses called reeds. Kaila took her small hands and parted some of the reeds so she could sneak a glimpse of this river she had been hearing about. At first sight Kaila actually felt faint. Shaking with surprise, she gazed with wonderment at the beauty of the river. The glowing sight of the sun sparkling on the water almost took her breath away. The sun!! "Yes," Kaila thought, "that must be the sunshine creating all that wonderful light." It hurt her eyes to keep looking at the sparkling water, so with great sadness Kaila let go of the reeds and slowly returned to the familiar surroundings of the forest.

Kaila tried to venture daily to the edge of the river. Most days she made it there unless one of her mud family trapped her up inside her dark house to abuse her. Sometimes she stayed at home because she sensed something dreadful was about to happen and thought she might be needed to help someone. Although she was just a small child, she felt guilty when she left her family to go to the river. Many times her gut feelings served her well, as terrifying things did happen. She knew she was being true to her mud family by staying there to take her share of the abuse. She felt overwhelmed when violence exploded around her, but she somehow always managed, even in her powerlessness, to help the ones in her family she so loved and cared for. So, the thought of not being there to help them frightened her more than the actual abuse she witnessed and often received.

One afternoon, Kaila was playing by the river's edge. She was making mud pies as usual because mud was all she had to play with. Kaila felt happy playing there because she loved being so close to the river. She did feel a gnawing sense of loneliness, but at least no one was around to hurt her.

The Mud People

✧

Every once in a while Kaila would stop playing and part the reeds so she could get a glimpse of the beautiful river. She could now enjoy watching the rhythmic movement of the river for longer periods of time without the sun hurting her eyes. She thought about what it might be like to feel the flow of the river washing over her. She wondered if this water could actually wash away her filth and mud. From the very first time she saw the sparkling water, Kaila sensed that there was something very different and special about it. It was not at all like the muddy water of the forest or even the water at her house. At home the water never seemed to get her clean. In the morning, after taking her bath the night before, she was always still covered with dirt and mud. Sometimes there was even a new layer of mud on her when she awoke! She was never quite sure how that happened. No, this water she saw before her was different, and it seemed to be inviting Kaila to do something, but she didn't know what.

As she sat enjoying the river and the sunshine, she suddenly felt someone's presence nearby. Terrified, Kaila gathered all her courage to look up and see who was there. As she peered up, she saw a strange-looking person standing a few feet away, smiling down at her. Kaila's first instinct was to run as fast as she could, yet a part of her felt fascinated by his appearance. Kaila jumped up quickly and shouted, "Who are you? What do you want? How did you find me? Are you going to hurt me? Does this river belong to you? I wasn't going to hurt it or take it. Why do you look so strange? Do you speak English? Why do you wear a dress, and how come you have hair hanging off your face? And why . . ."

Kaila was caught up in a whirlwind of questions, and she yelled them out one by one because of the intensity of her fear. She couldn't even stop talking long enough to allow this strange person to answer. When she was finally out of breath (but by no means questions), the stranger had a chance to introduce himself.

"Whoa, whoa, child, I'm sorry I scared you. My name is Juta and, no, I'm not here to hurt you. Yes, I do speak English. I come from a magical land far from here. I stopped by to meet you because I'd like to get to know you and be your friend."

"Friend," yelped Kaila, "no one *big* is a friend. All big people do is hurt me, and I don't need any more friends like that!"

"Yes, I know you have been hurt very much by big people. I'd like to show you that not *all* big people intend to hurt you. As a matter of fact, I am here to help you."

"I don't need your help. I'm able to take care of myself and even some of my mud family, thank you. What did you say your name was again? Why are you wearing a dress?"

"My name is Juta."

"That's a strange name. What does it mean?"

"Juta stands for wise teacher."

"Oh. What do you teach?"

"I help people, especially young ones like yourself, to find the real truth about themselves and the things around them. For example, tell me, please, what you know to be true about the Mystical River and sunshine."

"What do you mean Mystical River? Why do you call it 'mystical'?"

"You will discover its meaning for yourself soon."

"How will that happen, Juta?"

"It begins now by your telling me what you know to be true about the sunshine and Mystical River."

"Well, for one thing, Juta, I can't step out directly into the sunshine or I will burn up and I will die. I don't know how to swim, so if I step on the other side of these reeds I'll drown!"

"Who told you these things?"

"Why, my mud mother, of course, and she must be right because I'm the only one in my family to ever leave the deep shadows of the forest and come this close to the river and sunshine. And I already knew I can't swim because I can't."

"You are a very brave child," said Juta, "already searching for your own truth."

What Juta had just said made Kaila feel odd. No one had ever spoken to her in a way that made her feel there was goodness in her.

"What would happen if what you were told about the sunshine turned out not to be the truth?" he asked.

Kaila did not know how to answer Juta. All she knew about truth was what she had been taught by her mud family. She looked into Juta's eyes and saw they were filled with gentleness. She was still very confused about this Juta person, yet she didn't feel afraid of him.

"Perhaps today is a good day to begin a lesson on learning a different truth about the sunshine and river!" he said.

Juta stepped out from behind the reeds. He moved boldly into the river and the bright sunshine. Kaila screamed, covered her eyes, and fell to the ground. She just knew that Juta would burn up in the sunshine. She knelt there in the mud, shaking with fear for what seemed like a very long time. Suddenly, she heard someone calling her name.

"Kaila, Kaila, will you please uncover your eyes and look up at me?"

Kaila knew it was Juta's voice, but by now he surely must be charred! Slowly she uncovered her eyes and looked up. There, right before her eyes, was Juta, standing on the other side of the reeds, alive and well! The sunshine on his face made it glow with a golden luster. He was smiling at Kaila and his eyes glistened.

Juta stepped out of the river and back onto the muddy side of the reeds with Kaila. Kaila could not move from where she knelt. She was spellbound by what she had just seen Juta do . . . return from the bright sunlight unharmed.

"Would you like to step out into the sunshine and the soothing river with me, Kaila?" Juta asked. "The water here at the edge is always ankle deep, so you don't need to know how to swim."

Without looking up at him, Kaila shook her head no. She was feeling confused. Her body felt very heavy and she was beginning to tremble. She hated it when her body quivered and shook. It made her feel weak and vulnerable.

"Who is this Juta?" Kaila wondered. "Is there a different truth to life than what I know? Maybe he is an evil wizard in disguise sent here by my family to trick me. Perhaps they discovered that I have been leaving the forest and playing by the river and now they are going to teach me a lesson by tricking me into the sunshine with Juta's help."

Kaila heard a very stern and mean voice from within shouting at her. "No more thinking, no feeling, and no changing!" Yes—there could be no changing. That was another rule of her mud family. Kaila jumped up, and without a glance or word to Juta she ran back into the sunless forest, all the way home.

CHAPTER 2

Her First Steps to Freedom

*S*everal days had passed since Kaila met Juta at the river. As a matter of fact she had not been back since; this was partly because she had been locked up inside her dark house and abused by a member of her mud family. Also, she didn't know what to make of this giant of a man she had met. She had asked herself over and over again, "Did I really meet a wise teacher who stepped out into the beautiful river and sunshine?" Perhaps she had made it all up because she needed to believe in something beyond her own darkness, pain, loneliness, and mud.

Kaila feared she would never see the wise teacher

again. She had not even said goodbye to him when she abruptly left him at the river. Surely, even if he did exist, he would not want anything to do with a rude, muddy little girl. Kaila felt ashamed and all alone.

One day Kaila could stand it no longer. She missed playing down by the river and peeking through the reeds to see the beautiful water. Even if she never saw Juta again she could at least enjoy the rhythmic movement of the sparkling river and dream of being as clean as the clear water. Her longing became irresistible and she found herself running through the dark forest to the river.

When she arrived at her favorite spot she stopped suddenly. There at the reeds, looking out at the river, was Juta. Kaila felt no fear when she saw him. She was already out of breath from running so fast, and her heart started pounding from the excitement of seeing Juta. Since so much time had passed, she was relieved that Juta really did exist. She looked around quickly to see if anyone else was there. "Juta must be visiting with someone," she thought. "Why else would he be here?" But she saw no one.

After Kaila was able to catch her breath, she moved closer to Juta. Not too close, though. She wanted to leave herself room to flee if needed. After all, she wasn't completely sure about Juta, and he was still wearing that dress! When Kaila felt ready, she called his name.

"Juta, Juta, hello, it's me, Kaila."

Juta turned around slowly so he wouldn't frighten the young child.

"Hello, Kaila," he replied. "I'm so happy to see you again."

Juta's face glowed with the same brightness it had shown the day he had stepped out into the sunshine. This amazed Kaila because he was standing on the dark side of the reeds. It was clearly a mystery.

"Are you waiting for someone?" inquired Kaila.

"Yes," replied Juta.

"Have you been waiting long?" asked Kaila.

"I wait for as long as it takes," Juta answered.

"Well I hope you won't have to wait much longer," said Kaila. "Waiting is hard."

"My waiting is over," said Juta, "it was *you* I was waiting for."

"Me!" gasped Kaila. "You have been waiting for me?"

"Yes," replied Juta, "I have been waiting for you."

"How long have you been here?" asked Kaila in disbelief.

"I never left," said Juta.

Kaila was filled with joy. No one had ever wanted

to be with her before. She held her breath and closed her eyes tightly so she could hold on for as long as she could to this special feeling of being wanted. She needed to remember this incredible moment forever, especially when she was back with her mud family, where she never felt quite wanted.

Kaila looked up and shyly asked, "Why? Why, Juta, would you wait for a dirty little mud child like me?"

Juta smiled at Kaila. Love and compassion for her shone in his eyes.

"Kaila," said Juta softly, "you are not the only little child who is covered with filth and mud."

"I'm not?"

"No," said Juta, "there are many more who are covered with mud."

"Oh, you mean my mud family and neighbors."

"Not only them, Kaila, but there are others. Some are younger than you, some are older, some are much older. Some have more mud than you, some have less. Although you feel all alone in your muddy condition, you are not. And, Kaila, even if you see yourself as a dirty little mud child, you are very much worth waiting for."

Kaila loved it when Juta spoke to her that way. It made her feel so warm inside, and it somehow lessened the pain.

❧

"Have you ever been covered with mud?" asked Kaila.

"Yes," responded Juta, "I, like you, was once covered with mud."

"Did you look and feel as awful as I do?"

Juta laughed softly. "My mud was a little different from yours and came to cover me for different reasons. However, it was no less uncomfortable and painful."

"But yours is all gone," Kaila cried.

"Yes," said Juta, "mine is all gone."

Kaila could not imagine Juta covered with mud. She wondered who had been mean to such a kind teacher. But, more than that, she wondered how he came to be free of his mud. She wanted to ask him but felt afraid. She had a funny feeling it might have something to do with stepping into the river and sunshine. She was still absorbed in her thoughts when Juta asked, "Kaila, would you like to be free of *your* mud?"

"Oh, more than anything, I would! It is so confining, uncomfortable, and painful. Oh, Juta, is this why you have come from far away and waited so long for me? You are here to take my mud off, aren't you, Juta?"

Kaila looked up into the wise teacher's eyes with so

much hope and longing that it was difficult for Juta to answer. He knew how hard it would be for Kaila to hear what he had to say.

"No, Kaila, I am not here to remove your mud from you. Only you can do that. However, I can tell you how you can get your mud off. This is why I have come here, Kaila. I have been waiting a long time for this moment, to teach you how you can get your mud removed."

Kaila felt hurt and very disappointed. She had hoped Juta would have some magical power that could remove her mud. After all, he said he came from a magical land, and he did step out into the sunshine and river and live. Surely he must know of a way to help remove the mud from a helpless child. Kaila didn't know if she could even bear to hear what Juta had waited so long to tell her.

Just then, Kaila heard that soft gentle voice of her inner friend whisper, "Yes, listen." "Well, why not?" agreed Kaila. "Juta has been so kind and gentle with me. He hasn't tried to hurt me, and for the first time I have felt worth something to somebody. I guess it can't hurt to hear what he has to say. Besides, I don't have to do what he says. After all, I have left myself an out, and if I need to run I can. Juta may be a wise teacher, but I can outrun him. I'm good at running and hiding. I owe this to my mud family."

❖

Finally, after all her musing, Kaila took a deep breath and said, "OK, Juta, I would like you to teach me how I can get my mud off. I know I have wanted for a long time to be clean and free. Yes, oh yes, Juta, please do tell me!"

"To begin with, Kaila, you will need to be very brave and strong. You are already, Kaila, but you will need to be even more so."

Kaila listened closely to every word Juta spoke.

"Next, you must be willing to take some risks, to do some things you have never done before."

"Like what?" she asked.

"Well, child, in order to be freed of your mud, you must be willing to take a journey on the Mystical River to visit the Great Spirit of the Falls."

"Oh," screamed Kaila, jumping back, "I can't possibly do that! I already told you, I can't swim and I can't step into the direct sunshine or I'll burn up. You must have forgotten that I told you that, Juta. No, no, no, there must be another way. Oh, please, Juta, you must think of another way."

Kaila sat down on the hard muddy ground and began to cry. The darkness of the forest seemed to be inside her now, and it was getting darker and darker. She felt completely defeated and hopeless. She also felt great anger toward Juta. How could he expect someone as young as she to risk taking a journey on the Mystical River? He had stepped out into the sunshine and lived, but that didn't mean *she* could.

Juta sat down beside Kaila and said gently, "Kaila, you must be very afraid at the idea of taking a journey. I know you were told that the sunshine will burn you up if you step out into it, but, Kaila, it won't. You may have been told that to keep you from changing."

Juta paused for a moment to let Kaila think about what he had said.

"I believe in you, Kaila. I believe you can make a journey down the Mystical River to the Great Spirit of the Falls. If you listen closely, your inner friend will guide you and also reassure you that you can do it. I believe in you, Kaila. Will you try and believe in me?"

"Is the river ankle deep everywhere?"

"No," answered Juta. "It has places where it gets quite deep. But, Kaila, don't be afraid. Come and see what I brought to help you take your journey."

Together they walked over to the reeds. Juta parted the reeds, and there on the river about ten yards from them sat a small wooden boat.

"On your journey, Kaila, that boat will be a friend to you. The river from here to the boat is always ankle deep, so you don't have to swim to reach the boat. You can walk there. Kaila, you only have to choose to take a risk and go on your journey. Sometimes, child, the only thing that can help us get what we need and want is to take a risk. Are you willing to go after your dream of being without your mud? Are you willing to take a risk, Kaila?"

Kaila was feeling overwhelmed. It took her some time to control herself so she could answer Juta.

"Juta, I'm too little to row a boat, especially all by myself."

"You don't need to row that boat," Juta assured her. "It has no oars."

"No oars!" exclaimed Kaila.

Kaila felt herself getting light-headed, so she sat back down on the muddy ground. She was afraid of fainting in front of Juta. She would feel so embarrassed and ashamed if that happened. For whatever reason, Juta believed she could do it, and she didn't want to disappoint him.

"Yes," said Juta, "no oars. Once you are in the boat, the rhythmic flow of the river will guide you to the Great Spirit of the Falls. All you have to do is just enjoy the ride. It is very relaxing."

"But what if something happens and the boat turns over," wailed Kaila. "I'll drown for sure!"

"The flow of the river does become swift at times," Juta allowed, "and this may frighten you. However, there are two little handles in the boat to hold on to if you need them. Also, I'd like to give you this to wear on your journey."

Juta handed Kaila a small life jacket.

"What is this?" asked Kaila.

"It is a jacket that will help protect you. If, for any reason, you do become separated from the boat, this jacket will keep you afloat and you will not drown. It is important that you take it along on your journey and wear it at all times. And, Kaila, if you need me, I will be close by. Just call me."

Kaila had some final questions.

"Who is this Great Spirit of the Falls? How will I know when I am there? Is the Great Spirit someone I can trust? I'm very scared of strangers."

"The Great Spirit of the Falls is a very wise teacher," replied Juta. "The Spirit has the power to remove your mud with truth and love. You need not be afraid, Kaila. When you meet the Great Spirit you will come to know that you are not strangers to each other. The Spirit has always known and loved you.

"You will know you are there when you first hear the roar of the Great Falls. Then, you will see it. It might scare you, but trust me, please, Kaila, you will be safe. The Great Spirit will come to you under the Falls and the boat will take you there."

Kaila put her face in her hands and began to cry again. She was overwhelmed at the thought of all that stood before her: the journey, the boat, the life jacket, the Great Spirit of the Falls, Juta—the whole thing. Although she understood what Juta had told her, it seemed so big she didn't know what to make of it all. Right now her mud seemed safe, as did the shadows of the forest behind her and her mud family. Even the abuse seemed safe. Juta had not tricked her thus far, and she was beginning to feel like she might be able to trust him. Kaila felt completely exhausted when at last she heard someone talking to her. Softly from within she heard the gentle voice of her inner friend speaking.

"Kaila, you *can* make your journey. Just take it one step at a time. If you really want to be free of the mud, your great longing will bring you to your place of freedom. Trust! Trust first in yourself and trust in Juta. Trust in the Mystical River. It has been calling you for a long time now."

"What do I do?" Kaila thought. "If I stay here I will never get my mud off. If I go on this journey and something goes wrong I will at least know I had enough spunk to try."

Kaila got up, parted the reeds, and stepped into the ankle-deep water. She was so intent now on making her journey that she momentarily forgot Juta! However, Juta had far from forgotten Kaila. He was standing on the muddy side of the reeds smiling down at her. Tears were running down his face as he witnessed a very courageous young mud child taking her first steps to freedom!

CHAPTER 3

A Choice to Be Made

Kaila was completely fascinated by the rhythm of the Mystical River. It was swirling around and around her ankles. Watching this movement made her giggle and laugh, and she felt lighthearted and playful. It had been such a long while since she felt like a little child. As a matter of fact, when she began to giggle it frightened her. It took her a minute to recognize that the playful noise she was making was the sound of her own laughter.

Although Kaila could not yet feel the water on her ankles, she sensed that the Mystical River was already beginning to soften the hard mud. She felt if she stood there just a little longer she might be able to bend her feet. She started to giggle again and it felt wonderful!

Suddenly Kaila heard that very stern voice from within her inner self shouting at her. She hated this harsh voice that sometimes yelled at her. It was nothing like the other inner voice that spoke to her with hope about the Mystical River. She covered her ears in an attempt to block out its message. It did no good, though; this particular voice was used to being in control of Kaila.

"Kaila, you foolish, foolish child. Look where you are! Do you not know that the sun is about to burn you up? Quick, jump back on the muddy side where you belong before it is too late. It would help you to remember one of the safe rules of your mud family: no having any fun. Your playfulness is about to kill you. You don't even realize the danger you are in! When will you learn that the rules of your mud family are for your own good and safety? You must let them continue to control you."

"No," Kaila cried, "I won't go back to the muddy side of the reeds! I'm going on a journey down this Mystical River to get my mud off. I *am* going to go even if I do get burned up by the sun. If I do die I will at least be out of my misery of this awful dried mud. I won't let myself listen to you and change my mind. I'm going!"

And so, Kaila began moving toward the boat. This was another part of her that she didn't even know existed. It was a very determined part, a part that was helping her move right now even though she felt almost crippled with fear. Kaila felt like she was almost a completely different person. She had no idea she could be so determined.

Around her mud family Kaila felt mostly weak and fearful. The abuse she witnessed at her house frightened her so much that she couldn't be brave there. She only knew how to act like a victim, helpless like the rest of them. Now she hoped this determined part would stay with her a little while longer, as she was only halfway to the boat.

Again she heard the mean, rigid voice coming from her inner self.

"Kaila, how selfish can you be? Are you going to go off and leave your mud family all alone? What if they need you? Worse yet, what if your older mud sister Reeny needs you? You know how sick she is. Are you so set on taking your journey that you would even leave Reeny? Who is teaching you to be so selfish and to forget all the rules of your mud family? Do you think Reeny would abandon you if you were sick?

Who will help her while you are gone? And besides, how do you know all of this is going to work anyway? You actually trust a strange-looking person wearing a dress?"

Kaila could stand to hear no more. She stopped moving toward the boat. She was beginning to listen to that harsh voice of her inner self. "The voice is right," she thought. How stupid and selfish she was being. What had she been thinking? One of the most important people in her life was her mud sister Reeny. And no, Reeny would not go off and leave her if she were sick. Yes, the rules of her mud family must be true! Her foolish thinking and feelings had caused her to forget her family. She had almost let herself believe that she could actually go on a journey and come back mud free.

All Kaila's longing and hopeful expectations about being clean and without mud had now turned into utter despair and grief. Kaila's whole being was filled with pain.

With that, she turned around to head back home. She had a real need now to go and see Reeny.

However, standing only a few feet away from Kaila was Juta. He had been praying for her, as he knew she would encounter such obstacles in taking her journey.

Juta stood there in silence, looking down at Kaila. She quickly ran to his side.

"Oh, Juta," she sobbed. "I can't make this journey you have been talking about. I would have to leave my mud family. I can't possibly go off and leave them all alone. They need me, especially one of my older sisters. Her name is Reeny, and she is very sick. I must run back now and see her."

Tears were running down Kaila's mud face as she looked up into Juta's eyes. The pain of disappointment and sadness she was feeling deep inside was almost more than she could stand.

"Kaila," Juta began, "the harsh voice that speaks now is not your inner friend. This part is trying to trick you into not taking your journey by playing mind games with you."

"Mind games?" asked Kaila.

"Yes," replied Juta. "Mind games. The very best way you can help your mud family is by taking your journey. Your strength will be a light to them and many others. Because of your journey, some of your mud family will decide to take the journey also. Then they, like you, can experience the freedom and peace of being without their mud. You are not being selfish by taking your journey, Kaila. You are simply responding to the true self that is within you. Your true self is not very strong yet, so it is hard for you to hear it clearly. It will become stronger as you take your journey. You'll have to choose, Kaila, which voice you will listen to and allow to control you."

She stood there looking down into the Mystical River. Its rhythmic flow did not seem to hold any fascination at all now. She was feeling too confused about what Juta had just said to even notice the movement of the river. Just exactly what was a true self? Was it part of that gentle, kind voice she also heard from within her inner self? Was it the part that had first told her there was more to life than what she had experienced in the dark forest? And what exactly had Juta meant when he said she would have to choose which self she wanted to control her? She thought, "Could it be that I could take control of my *own* life by making a choice? I certainly had no control over the abuse that had happened to me or this awful mud that covers my body so I can hardly move."

Kaila's head was starting to hurt from thinking so much! The thoughts of giving up her dreams of being clean and without mud continued to make her feel very sad. She wanted to believe Juta, that taking her journey would be a real way of helping her mud family. But what about her sister Reeny? How could she go and leave her behind? Reeny depended on her help.

"Juta, I can't go and leave Reeny all by herself."

"Do you think Reeny would want you to give up your chance of being free of your mud, Kaila?"

"No, she would want me to go if it meant I could be free of my mud. She, more than the rest of my mud family, knows how much I hate being covered with it."

"Do you believe your journey means you will be able to get free of your mud, Kaila?" asked Juta.

"I thought it did. But I'm not sure now."

"Why don't you ask your true inner friend?" Juta urged.

With that Kaila grew very still. Slowly she heard that gentle voice speaking to her from within.

"Kaila, do not be so quick to give up your dream . . . your dream of being clean. You have just told Juta that Reeny would want you to take your journey if it meant freedom from your mud. She would be the first one to tell you to go and not to worry about her. So that harsh voice that tries to control you is for sure your false self. It tries to keep you from changing by stirring up fear within you. By choosing your journey you will be learning for the first time how to love and take care of yourself. This love will cast out the fear of your false self. In learning this, you will have a very powerful gift to give others. Most people like you who are covered with mud do not know how to love themselves. Go, Kaila, go now and do not look back."

Kaila knew her inner friend was right. She hugged Juta goodbye and turned around toward the boat that awaited her. Nothing would stop her now. Her determined self was back in control. She felt lighthearted again and was thankful to have her dream back. "Yes," she thought, "I can be in control of my own life by making a choice to take my journey." She thought again of Reeny, and this made her feel sad. However, Reeny would be so surprised, happy, and proud of her for making her journey. She grew excited thinking about how wonderful it would be for Reeny and the rest of her mud family to see her without her mud. They would then know it was possible for all of them also to be free and clean. She just knew Reeny would be the first one to decide to take her own journey after she saw how pretty Kaila was without her mud. Yes, Juta was right: taking this journey was by far the best way to help her mud family.

Kaila had now reached the boat, and without a second thought she took a big leap and landed right in the middle of it. She felt so proud of herself—she had actually taken a risk and made a choice to do something, even if she wasn't quite sure how it would turn out.

She lay down in the boat to rest a minute and she heard herself laughing and giggling again. She felt the rhythm of the Mystical River slowly start the boat moving. She was finally on her way, and there was no stopping her now. She just giggled and giggled and felt strangely warm and peaceful inside.

CHAPTER 4

A Happening on the River

Oh my, I must have fallen asleep! Where am I?! What has happened to me? I can hardly breathe," Kaila worried as she sailed along in her little boat.

"Wait, Kaila, wait. Try and remember," whispered her inner friend.

"Oh, I know, I'm on my journey to get my mud off. It's OK, I'm safe. This boat is my friend. Hooray, I'm going to get my mud off! I'm glad these handles are here so I can pull myself up. Oops, it's hard to get a grip on them with all this mud on my hands. Up I go!"

With that Kaila pulled herself up so she could see exactly where she was on the Mystical River.

"Oh look, look what I can see! Is this a dream? The sky is such a beautiful blue and there is so much of it. And look, over there, all along the river, the prettiest wildflowers I have ever seen. I never knew the world had so many colors and flowers. My mud mother would be so happy if I could take her some of these wonderful flowers. Then everything would be OK at my house. I bet she would like me a lot if I could just find a way to make her feel better. My mud dad would for sure be better, and everyone would talk to each other, and we would have lots of fun and would be a very warm and happy family. I know, once I get my mud off, I'll pick some of those beautiful flowers and take them home. It will make everyone feel happy, and then I'll be really loved."

Kaila was slowly feeling alive. The sights and sounds filled her with much wonderment and joy. Experiencing all this newness in her world gave her some relief from the pain and hopelessness she felt almost every day. It had a way of numbing the harsh reality of her little existence, and she found herself laughing and actually happy to be alive.

Her tremendous fear, at least for the present, was not controlling her. Her body was actually relaxing, and at times she was unaware of the mud.

"I never knew birds could make such pretty music.

The Mud People

❖

The songs they whistle sound so happy. I wish I could whistle like they do. My mud dad knows how to whistle. Sometimes when he feels happy and my mud mother isn't yelling or acting crazy, he enjoys whistling. I wonder if the birds taught him how to whistle?

"What was that over there in the reeds? It looked like a mud person like me! Look, there again, there is another one. Juta was right, there are other mud people besides my mud family. And another! That one was a little like me, and her eyes looked so sad. I hope all these mud people will one day take a journey to get their mud removed."

Kaila was completely captivated by all the different mud people she saw. Every once in a while, on either side of the Mystical River, someone would part the reeds and look out at her. She would wave to them, and she somehow felt a bonding with these mud people even though she didn't know who they were. She especially liked to see the little ones her own age. She tried to guess by their size how old they were. It gave her a sense she was not alone, and for the first time she knew she was not different from everyone else. There were actually others like herself.

Kaila bent over the side of the boat to look into the beautiful Mystical River. She felt frightened by what she saw looking back at her. She slowly realized it was her image she was looking at. She looked like a scary monster, an ugly, scary monster. All that even resembled a little girl were her eyes. She felt thankful that her eyes were not covered with mud.

Kaila began to daydream about what she would look like after her mud was gone. All of a sudden the boat began to sway back and forth. The movement of the river had changed and she felt frightened. Kaila thought for sure the boat would tip over. Slowly her body became very heavy and she began to shake. She straightened up and quickly slipped her hands back into the handles. She glanced down and her worst fear came true! She had forgotten to bring the life jacket Juta had given her to help keep her safe! Her shaking became uncontrollable and she managed to lie back down in the boat to keep it from tipping over.

Kaila became paralyzed with fear. Her body was shaking out of control. It was as if she were having a seizure. The current of the river seemed to be getting even rougher, and she just knew the boat would tip over and she would die.

"How could I have been so stupid? Juta warned me to take along the life jacket. I deserve to die! I'm too ashamed to even cry to Juta for help. If he came to help me he would holler and yell at me for not doing

as he told me. Worse yet, he may tease me and make fun of me. Suppose Juta knew I would forget my life jacket? Maybe this was all a trick of Juta's to get me out on this river all by myself. I'm completely helpless now and Juta could come and abuse me! Help, please, someone help me!"

At once the current of the river became calm again, and Kaila almost instantaneously stopped shaking. She opened her eyes and looked up to find Juta smiling down at her. He was sitting in a boat right beside her. His hand was resting on hers. Juta slowly helped Kaila to sit up. She was exhausted and terrified.

Kaila was too frightened to speak. She didn't know where Juta had come from. She hadn't heard him pull up next to her. She only knew that right after she managed to scream for help, Juta was there. Was he here to help or to take advantage of her?

"I thought you might need this, Kaila. You left it behind in your hurry to get to the boat. Please take it and put it on. It will help you stay safe. As you can feel, the river is getting rougher. You're not far from the falls now."

With that Juta handed Kaila the life jacket! Kaila reached out her mud hands to take the jacket from Juta. She felt herself half in shock from the terror she had just experienced and half in disbelief that Juta was there beside her. She heard that gentle voice of her inner friend begin talking to her, which helped bring her out of her stupor.

"You see Kaila, it is OK to trust Juta. He really is your friend and helper. He came to help you as soon as you called, just as he told you he would. Your safety is very important to Juta. He will not harm you."

With that, Kaila finally managed to speak.

"Oh, Juta, I'm very happy to see you! I was so frightened that the boat would tip over and I would drown. I was afraid to call to you for help because I thought you would really be angry with me for forgetting the life jacket and you might abuse me."

Juta threw back his head and let out a big hearty laugh. It was very hard for Kaila to understand because it wasn't the sound of a mocking laugh, or the kind of laugh some of her mud family made when she said something stupid or made a mistake. It was a joyous kind of laugh. It filled the air with its gaiety, and even the Mystical River seemed to absorb it. As a matter of fact, it made Kaila laugh. She found herself laughing and laughing, and all the fear and terror that was held in her body began to lift. When they had both stopped laughing Kaila felt very light-headed and happy.

"Juta, why were you laughing?" asked Kaila.

"Your fear that I would hurt you made me laugh. You see, Kaila, there is no part of me that would ever abuse you. I know this is hard for you to trust and believe, but, Kaila, I could never hurt you. I heard your cry for help and I came. You are very precious to me!"

Kaila was still struggling within herself to believe him.

"It won't be long now, Kaila, before you will be at the falls. May I urge you to put on the life jacket? It will help to keep you safe, and I will be close by. Call if you need me."

And Juta was gone!

"Will I ever be old enough to understand who Juta is?" wondered Kaila. "Will I wake up one day and find that I have dreamt this whole thing? If this is a dream, I pray I won't wake up, ever. I want to trust and believe in Juta. He wasn't even mad at me because I forgot the life jacket. He didn't scold me, mock me, shame me, hurt me, or take advantage of my small-ness. He was kind and gentle and acted as if it was even OK that I had forgotten the jacket. He seemed to understand that in my struggle to make the choice to go on the journey, it was no wonder I forgot the jacket! After all, it's not every day I have to make such a big choice. As a matter of fact, this is the first time anyone gave me a choice about anything, and I wanted to choose like I was big and knew what I was doing. Could that mean Juta might even like me, I mean like me even when I do things wrong? I've never known a love like that before."

Suddenly, Kaila became aware of the sound of the roar of the falls. It startled her. She had no idea how long she had been thinking about Juta or how far she had traveled down the Mystical River. She only knew she had to get the life jacket on quickly, as the falls sounded very near. Her mud hands were shaking as she struggled to get it on and secured. "It's not easy to do things with your hands covered with mud," Kaila thought.

She had no sooner fastened the jacket when she realized she was inches away from the falls. The sound was almost deafening! She quickly put her mud hands on the handles of the boat. In no time the boat was going over the falls. When she saw all the water around her and felt the swiftness of it, she panicked, let go of the handles, and covered her eyes. Her body flew up and she was pushed by the current into the front of the boat. She grabbed the sides of the boat, but the pressure of the water was very strong, and her hands were torn from the boat and she felt her body being lifted out. It was then that she felt a force like a strong hand on her back, holding her in the boat. She wondered if it was Juta.

Kaila fainted from sheer fright, only to awaken later lying inside the wooden boat, which had come safely to rest under the falls. She closed her eyes and went to sleep knowing somehow she had made it and was once again, for the time being, safe!

CHAPTER 5

The Cleansing

Slowly Kaila opened her eyes and thought, "I must be one year older because my mud body feels as if it has been sleeping for a very long time. I feel frightened because I don't know what time of day it is, or even what *day* it is. How long have I been gone? Does my mud family even know I've been away? I know Reeny would miss me. My mud mother might feel happy I was gone because I would be one less mud child to have to care for. Well, I guess I could at least sit up and see where I am."

Kaila pulled herself up and slowly looked around. She sensed she was in a very special place. She loved the fact that right above her head a very powerful falls was flowing. It didn't frighten her in the least. She couldn't feel the dampness of the spray that showered her because her mud was too thick, though it did appear to soften the hardness of the mud, and she was very thankful for that. She also observed happily that even under these Mystical Falls the sun seemed to be shining everywhere. She couldn't understand how this could be, and since it made her head hurt to try to figure it out, she was content to let this beautiful mystical light chase away all darkness.

"Juta, Juta, is that you?"

Kaila had spotted Juta sitting not far from her. She had no idea what he was doing. His legs were crossed in front of him, his eyes were closed, and his hands rested palms up on his folded legs. Kaila thought it a very funny way to sleep. She was pleased, as always, to see Juta. What a wonderful friend she had in Juta. She hoped he wouldn't mind if she called him her friend.

Again Kaila called. "Juta, Juta, please, will you wake up now?"

Slowly Juta opened his eyes. He did not want to frighten the little mud child.

"Hello, Kaila, how are you feeling?"

"Oh, Juta, I'm fine, a little stiff and sore, but I'm used to that with all this mud on me. Thank you, Juta, for staying with me on the journey here. I'm relieved to see you, and I'm sorry for waking you up."

"I'll never leave you, Kaila, and there's no need to be sorry. I wasn't sleeping."

"You weren't? What were you doing, Juta? If it's OK for me to ask."

"It's always OK for you to ask me anything, anytime, Kaila. You are a very bright and curious child, and you learn much through your questions."

Kaila quickly looked down because she felt shame. She knew she was stupid and ugly because this is what she had always been told by her mud mother. She wondered why Juta didn't know that. He knew everything else, it seemed. Her thoughts were interrupted as she heard Juta explaining what he was doing.

"I never really sleep, Kaila. I just close my eyes, pray, and rest. This way if anyone should need me, I'm awake to help."

"But Juta, don't you get tired? Everyone needs sleep. When I'm hurting or afraid I always sleep. I can't begin to imagine being awake all the time."

"Yes, you are right, Kaila, sleeping does help with the pain and fear. It helps you enter a safe place within yourself where you get rest and strength for every new day. That's what I am doing, only I don't need to physically go to sleep to enter my safe place.

It's just something special I do so I can always be where I am needed quickly."

"Thank you for answering all my questions. You are a great teacher and friend, Juta! I mean, it's OK to call you my friend, isn't it?"

"Yes, Kaila, I have always been your friend, even before you knew me. I will always be your friend, teacher, and helper. Do you feel rested enough now, Kaila, to meet an even greater friend than I?"

"Oh yes, Juta. You mean the Great Spirit of the Falls?"

"Yes, Kaila. Are you ready to meet the Great Spirit?"

"Yes, I'm ready, but will you stay with me, please? I'm sort of frightened. The Spirit sounds so big and powerful, and I'm little. Sometimes, Juta, big people really scare me. Often big people hurt me or trick me and shame me. Please, can you stay with me, or do I have to brave the Big Spirit on my own?"

Juta let out a laugh and replied, "I'm staying right here with you, Kaila. Here, give me your hand, and I'll take you to the Great Spirit."

"Oh, no, Juta, the mud on my hands is rough and dirty. It will cause you pain to hold my hand. Maybe you'd rather wait till I get my hands clean."

"Your mud doesn't scare me, Kaila, and I'd gladly feel the pain of your mud just to hold your hand."

The Mud People

✧

Kaila looked up into Juta's eyes and she could see he meant what he said. He was for real. She somehow knew Juta felt the pain all over her body without even touching her. She wondered how he could do this. Slowly she slipped her tiny mud hand into Juta's big, strong hand. Juta just smiled down at her. He didn't even say ouch! Kaila also noticed Juta wasn't repulsed by her muddy condition.

Slowly Juta led Kaila to the other side of the falls.

"See over there, Kaila," Juta said, "where the mist gets a little heavier? There right in front of those rocks."

"Yes," said Kaila, "I see the mist."

"This is where the Great Spirit will speak to you," Juta said.

"Is that mist the Great Spirit, Juta?"

"No, Kaila, you will not really see the Great Spirit as you see me. The Great Spirit stays hidden, so as not to scare anyone. You see, Kaila, your eyes could not behold the brightness of the Great Spirit, for the light is so bright it would hurt your eyes. The Spirit uses different forms and places to enter, to safely hide its greatness."

"But, Juta, how will I know when the Spirit is hidden and ready to help me?"

"You will know. You will hear the voice of the Spirit coming from within you, and then you will feel the presence. Are you ready to meet the Great Spirit?"

"I guess so, Juta, but I must tell you I'm sort of confused and frightened."

"That's fine, Kaila. You are right where you need to be."

Juta closed his eyes and entered the safe place within himself. He quietly prayed for the Great Spirit to come. He had hardly begun to pray when he heard a strong and mighty wind enter the Mystical River and settle in the mist. It frightened Kaila, and she turned away from the mist and wrapped her mud arms around Juta's waist. Juta held the small child close and safe.

In a deep voice that seemed to fill the river and drown out the falls, Kaila heard, "Hello, my child, how very good and brave of you to come."

Kaila heard the voice and at first she thought it was Juta speaking. But when she opened her eyes Juta's were still closed and he was very still. Kaila closed her eyes and heard that strong papa-like voice once more.

"Don't be frightened, child, I won't hurt you. If you turn around and look over here at the mist, you will find me."

Kaila felt so frightened and unsure, she wanted

The Mud People

✦

Juta to help turn her around because she felt frozen in place. Juta was very still, but she could feel his love warming her body and giving her support. She still felt too frightened to turn around, and it was then she heard a second voice from within. It was a very gentle mama-like voice.

"Kaila," she said, "you are safe here with us, and we are pleased you were brave enough to make your journey. We are here to help you become the child you were meant to be, a beautiful child without your painful mud."

Kaila liked it that the mama-like voice called her by name. More than that she loved the gentle voice saying that Kaila was meant to be a beautiful child. How she hoped deep within that this was true. The mama-like voice was so kind and loving that Kaila overcame her fear. Slowly and very carefully, she turned around to face the mist.

It was beautiful! The mist was a shimmering bright light but not so bright she couldn't look at it. It was like looking at a huge crystal shining in the sun, and she couldn't remember ever having seen anything so beautiful before. The light was even prettier than the first time she beheld the Mystical River.

"Are you the Great Spirit?" Kaila asked.

"Yes," replied the papa-like voice.

Kaila felt a little confused at hearing two different voices speak for the Great Spirit.

"Are there two Great Spirits?" she asked.

"No, little one," replied Mama Spirit. "There is just one Great Spirit."

"Please don't get mad at me," begged Kaila, "but you sound like two different spirits to me. I'm sure I heard a papa-like voice and a mama-like voice. Am I not hearing right?"

"You are hearing just fine, Kaila. You see, the Great Spirit is both mother and father, both male and female. We are one and the same spirit, and whomever you need to speak to, whether Papa Spirit or Mama Spirit, will determine which one addresses you."

Kaila thought that it would be wonderful but confusing to be two things at once. She didn't think she really understood it all very well yet.

"How was your journey down the Mystical River, little one?" asked Papa Spirit.

"Oh, I loved being in that boat, drifting down the river, seeing and hearing all kinds of new things. And I saw other mud people just like me, and I heard birds whistling and I saw the most beautiful wildflowers and I forgot my life jacket and Juta came and helped me and . . ."

The Great Spirit began laughing and it scared

Kaila because it seemed to shake the whole falls. Besides, what was so funny? Hadn't the Great Spirit asked about her journey?

"I see you had a most exciting journey," Mama Spirit broke in. "Please forgive Papa Spirit for laughing. He sometimes forgets his manners. He wasn't making fun of you, Kaila. Your excitement and energy tickled his heart. He is very fond of little girls, especially those covered with mud."

"Wow," thought Kaila, "someone else besides Juta might like me, too! Can all this be real? Could I be loved even in my muddy condition?" she wondered.

"Are you rested enough to start your cleansing, Kaila?" asked Mama Spirit.

"Yes, oh yes, I can hardly wait. Please. I feel fine. I took a big nap when I got here. You can ask Juta."

"There's no need for me to ask Juta, Kaila. I believe you," said Mama Spirit.

Kaila didn't know what to think or feel because no one "big" had ever believed her before.

"By the way, do you know Juta?" Kaila asked.

"Yes," answered Papa Spirit, "we know Juta quite well. He is really one with us, which I know must sound a little confusing to you. Juta is very much connected to us."

Kaila turned to look at Juta, but he wasn't there. She immediately looked around for him, and she soon saw him a little ways away, sitting down with his knees crossed in front of him again. Kaila knew this time that Juta was in his safe place.

"I'm ready now, kind Spirit, to begin."

"All right, Kaila, we will begin your cleansing with your mind, which means we will start by removing the mud from your head, face, and neck. I'd like to ask you to just sit down where you are. That's right, get as comfortable as you can be with that awful mud on you. Now, let's begin.

"First, Kaila, please tell both me and Mama Spirit all the things you have been taught to think about yourself. It's not important to say who told you these things because we already know that. What's important is that you bring out into the light what *you* think about yourself so we can help you. Do you think you can do that for us?"

"Oh yes," Kaila assured him. "Do you want me to tell you everything at once, or one thing at a time?"

"Very good question, child. Please think one thought at a time and pause for a little bit in between. It will perhaps cause you pain to think of these things, but I promise we will help change that. You may begin now."

The Mud People

✦

"Well, first thing, I think I am very ugly.

"Next, I think I am very bad.

"I think there is something wrong with me because my mud mother hurts me so much and tells me *I* cause her to hurt me.

"I think I'm not worthy of love, or safety and closeness, because no one wants to give me those things. Even my mud dad leaves me.

"I think I should die because I cause bad things to happen.

"I think all the mud that covers me is my fault.

"Great Spirit," said Kaila, "my head hurts from thinking so much. That's because I'm not even supposed to be thinking."

Kaila grew very quiet. She began not only to think she was bad, but she started feeling bad. She felt she was betraying her family by thinking all these things and then saying them out loud to the Great Spirit. If her mud family heard any of this, not only would they abuse her when she got back home, they might send her away *forever*.

"What is it you are thinking right now, Kaila?" asked the gentle Mama Spirit. "You seem to be struggling with something."

"I feel very scared," said Kaila. "I don't think I should have told you all those things."

All at once Kaila heard that very mean voice from within her speak.

"Kaila, you will pay a great price for telling all these secrets to the Great Spirit. Just wait until you get home. Your mud mother will lock you up in the closet forever. You will not be allowed to ever go outside again and you will never again see Reeny if you continue. Don't you know you are making Reeny worse by letting the Great Spirit know your mud family secrets? How could you tell on your mud dad. You will hurt him very much if you keep telling. Stop now before it is too late."

Kaila brought her mud hands to her face and began to sob. She believed she was being so bad by telling her mud family secrets. She just wanted to lie down and *die.* There was a heaviness on Kaila and she knew she had felt as much as she could feel. She then felt an arm around her shoulders. She peeked through her hands to see Juta kneeling beside her.

"Juta, what am I doing? Am I betraying my mud family by talking with the Great Spirit? Am I getting my mud family in trouble with the Great Spirit? Will the Great Spirit hurt my mud family, especially my mud mother, who taught me to think so many of these things about myself? I don't want her to be hurt, Juta. She is my mud mother and I love her in spite of the abuse. Please don't let the Great Spirit hurt my mud mother or mud dad or any of my mud family. Please, Juta!"

"No one is going to hurt your mud family, Kaila. This is the false voice talking to you from within. It is going to try and stop you from going through with your cleansing. As you are set free from your mud, the false voice will have less and less power to control you, or even to speak to you. You are doing very well, Kaila, and everything is OK. The Great Spirit would never hurt anyone in your mud family because we love all of them, also. This is not about shame or fault, this is about healing and getting your mud off so you can know your truest self. If this is too much right now we can come back again some other time."

"Oh, no," Kaila pleaded, "I have waited long enough. I am going to go through this cleansing, no matter what, Juta. I just needed for you to tell me this is all OK, and that I'm not being bad by telling the mud secrets to the Great Spirit."

"Not only is it OK, Kaila, for you to bring the secrets out into the light, it is the very best thing to do, and no part of you is bad. You see, Kaila, another name for secrets is lies. They are things that are said to you so often that they begin to feel like the truth. But a lie is never the truth. So right now, this very first part of your cleansing is most important, because it will destroy all the power the lies have had over you. Can you trust me a little longer and keep going to get the mud off your mind? When it is off you will begin not only to think the truth, you will begin to experience it also."

Kaila looked deep into Juta's eyes, as she always did when she needed assurance. Once again, she knew she could trust him, for his eyes were filled with light and love for her.

"Great Spirit," Kaila announced, "I'm ready to continue."

"Is there anything else you can think of that you would like to bring out into the light?" Papa Spirit asked.

"I think I am mean and God will punish me because sometimes I wish my mud mother would die or go away because the abuse hurts so bad. I wish some of my mud sisters and my brother would go away too. I think I hate them sometimes because they are mean to me. I believe my mud dad hates me because he thinks I cause my mud mother to act crazy."

"Anything else, little one?"

"No, Great Spirit, I can't think of anything else!"

Mama Spirit had tears in her eyes. It caused her

great pain to think such a young child could hold such awful lies in her head about herself. She could not address Kaila even though she sensed it was her turn, so Papa Spirit gently spoke to the little child.

"Kaila, you have done very well. All you need to do now is sit still where you are, close your eyes, and be very brave. The mist you are looking at from where you hear my voice will become a pulsating mist, in order to remove the mud from your head, face, and neck. You will feel pain, especially once the top mud is off and as the mist gets closer to your hair, face, and neck. The pulsating mist will sting the skin, but know that when you begin to feel it, it is almost done. If ever it becomes too much, just yell stop and I will stop the cleansing at once. It is OK to stop and rest as many times as you need to. We are in no hurry here. Your safety and well-being come first. Do you understand this, Kaila?"

"Yes, Papa Spirit, I do understand, and even though I feel scared, I want to be free of my mud. I promise to be strong and brave."

"That you are, my child, that you are!

"All right, Kaila, we are ready to begin. Juta is close by. Now close your eyes and we will start."

Kaila closed her eyes tightly, and just as the Spirit was changing into the pulsating mist, she jumped up and shouted, "Wait, wait, Great Spirit, I forgot something!"

"What did you forget, child?"

"Oh, Great Spirit, I have a favor to ask you. Please, would it be all right with you if I could somehow get my hands cleansed, too? Once the mud is gone from my hair and face, I want to be able to feel them, but I won't be able to if my hands are still covered with mud. Please, is it too much to ask for in this first cleansing?"

"No, child, nothing you ask is ever too much. Yes, it will be just fine to have your hands freed. Just place them on your head. When you are ready again, just sit down and close your eyes."

With that Kaila sat back down and closed her eyes. She placed her hands on her mud head. She could hardly wait to know what it would be like without the mud. Slowly she heard a strong wind approaching and she felt a funny sensation on her hands first and then her head. It kept coming and coming, and she began to feel the pulse of the water more and more. Slowly, but surely, she began to experience pain on her hands, head, face, and neck. Faster and faster the water swirled around her. Then it really began to hurt as the mud was being literally chipped away. Her little heart started beating faster and faster, and she became afraid she wouldn't be brave enough to hold on. She started crying, but she did not yell stop! She was so determined to get through this. And just when Kaila felt she could take no more of the cleansing pain, it stopped. She felt a tear run down her cheek and she touched it with her finger. She opened her eyes and jumped up screaming . . .

"Juta, Juta, I can feel my face!"

Kaila was laughing and crying at the very same time. She quickly moved her hands from her face to her hair. Again she found herself shrieking with joy and excitement.

"Juta, Juta, look, I can feel my hair. The mud is gone! Come and feel how soft it is. Juta, it smells clean! That awful mud smell is gone. Hurry, Juta, hurry. Feel and smell my hair!"

Juta touched her soft face and bent over to smell her hair.

With that Kaila grew very quiet. Juta knew exactly what Kaila was thinking, but he also knew to wait. So, as always, Juta patiently waited for Kaila's question.

"Juta, can you see my hair as well as touch it?"

"Yes," said Juta, "I can."

"Then, Juta, can you also see my face?"

"Yes, Kaila, I can."

Kaila became still and she felt her body start to

shake. She felt scared to ask her question. She knew Juta did not lie, but she was afraid of the answer. After what seemed like a long time, Kaila finally asked, "Juta, am I ugly?"

Juta slowly slipped his hand into Kaila's clean hand. It startled Kaila at first because she was not used to anything really touching her. She looked up at Juta, and he said, "Come over here, Kaila, to this clear Mystical Puddle, where you will be able to see your reflection. I can tell you what a beautiful little girl you are, but I think you need to see for yourself."

As they stood in front of the Mystical Puddle, Kaila was almost frozen in fear. Now was a big moment of truth. She had to look at herself without the mud on her face. She began to shake and cry. Gently Juta knelt down by the puddle and looked in. He waited for Kaila to do the same. He would wait for as long as it took!

Kaila thought to herself, "I am so scared to look into the Mystical Puddle and see my real self. With all the mud on my face, I could tell myself it was that which made my mud mother tell me over and over again I was an ugly child. But what if I'm still just as ugly without my mud? I am so nervous, but I've come this far, and Juta didn't scream when he saw me, so maybe it isn't that bad."

The Mud People
✧

With that she knelt down beside Juta and shyly looked into the Mystical Puddle. What came first, Kaila couldn't remember. It happened so fast, she knew she was both screaming with joy and crying with relief.

"Juta, Juta," she kept screaming, "I see a little child in the water. Is that me?! Is the ugly scary monster gone? Is that my face looking back at me?"

Juta smiled. "You mean this one?" he inquired, bringing his hands to rest on Kaila's cheeks.

Kaila saw his hands on her face in the water and felt them on her cheeks. Before long, Juta's hands were covered with her tears of joy.

"Yes," sobbed Kaila, "I mean that one."

With that, Kaila turned to Juta and threw her mud arms around his neck. She hugged him very tightly, and Juta could feel all the excitement and relief in her body. Juta put his arms around Kaila's mud body and slowly rocked her. She fell fast asleep from all the excitement and joy.

When Kaila awoke, she was still resting in Juta's arms. She did not know how long she had napped, but it made her feel so loved because Juta had not put her down. He had held her the whole time in his arms. Juta was right. Not only could she now think the truth, but she was experiencing it. Ugly, scary, monster-looking little girls don't get held. She was not an ugly, scary, monster-looking little girl anymore, she was just a little girl.

Kaila slowly reached up her clean hand and stroked Juta's cheek. Juta smiled down on her.

"Are your arms tired, Juta, from holding me?"

"You are not heavy, Kaila, and I enjoy holding you. I'm glad you are learning you are safe with me. I know it is very hard for you to trust. My arms are always here for you. You are free to climb in and out anytime you need."

Kaila climbed out of Juta's arms and sat right next to him. She felt her face, over and over. She loved that her hands could feel things. Her hair felt soft and it still smelled clean. She felt so safe with Juta, and she was learning to trust and love him. His arms were the best, safest place she had ever been, and she knew he loved her because he had said she was welcome to climb in and out of his arms anytime. Juta did not think she was a bother. In fact he had told her so many times. That was one of the things she liked best about Juta. Kaila could not wait until her mud family met Juta and got all clean and nice smelling. She knew they wouldn't have to be one of the mud families in their neighborhood anymore. Speaking of mud . . .

"Juta."

"Yes, little one."

"I'm ready to find the Great Spirit again and get some more mud off."

"You know, Kaila, you have been through a lot of healing today, and you can come back as many times as you need to, until all your mud is gone. It might be better to wait and get some more rest. The second time down the Mystical River is much easier, because you know where you are going and you will not be filled with fear."

Kaila jumped up and cried.

"No way, Juta, I came to get *all* my mud off *now*. I have waited so long. Please, take me back to the Great Spirit. I have the rest of my life to rest. I want to be free!"

"OK, Kaila, I trust if you get too tired you will let us know. I just wanted to reassure you that this falls will always be here and there is no hurry for you to get all the mud off today."

"No hurry for you maybe, Juta, but my heart longs to be without the rest of this mud."

"Well, then, come, little one, it is your heart area that will be cleansed next. You are very special, Kaila."

Juta slipped his hand into Kaila's, and this time

Kaila wasn't as startled. Juta took her back in front of the Great Spirit.

"My, my, what a beautiful little girl I see standing in front of me, Mama Spirit. Can you see her?" asked Papa Spirit.

"Oh yes," said Mama Spirit, smiling. "I see her pretty face and shiny hair quite clearly."

Kaila let out an embarrassed giggle, which in turn made Papa Spirit giggle, which in turn shook the whole falls. Kaila was frightened by the shaking, and stopped laughing. Papa Spirit also stopped, because he saw fear in Kaila's eyes and realized he was indeed shaking the falls.

"Papa Spirit," Kaila said, "you have a very powerful laugh." She paused for a moment, looked up, and asked, "Know what?"

"No, what child?"

"My mud sister Reeny loves to laugh and so does my mud dad. Reeny says laughter is the best medicine. You must think so too, because you surely do know how to laugh."

That made Papa Spirit start laughing again, and Mama Spirit had to nudge him to get control so he wouldn't scare Kaila again.

"I'm ready to start the next cleansing now, Great Spirit."

The Mud People

"You are a very determined child," said Mama Spirit. "You most definitely have a strong spirit within you."

"You mean I have a spirit part like you, Mama Spirit?" Kaila asked in wonderment.

"Yes, Kaila, part of our spirit is in you and this is what has helped bring you to this place of healing."

Kaila wasn't sure what all that meant, but she knew she could ask Juta later. Papa Spirit spoke next.

"This time, Kaila, we want to cleanse your heart. It's what you feel about yourself. So once again we will need you to reveal to us, one at a time, everything you feel about yourself. It may be very painful, and I must ask you to try and feel as much of the pain as you are able. One cannot heal what one does not feel. Do you understand this, Kaila?" asked Papa Spirit.

"Yes, Papa Spirit, I think I do. I will try my very best to feel my pain, anger, fear, shame, and anything else. I'm a little scared of the cleansing mist."

"We understand that, Kaila," chimed in Mama Spirit. "Remember you can yell stop at any time and we will stop."

"Okay, I'm ready," said Kaila.

Kaila sat down and closed her eyes. She felt both excited and scared. She couldn't wait until her feelings were cleansed. Then her heart would be able to feel anytime and her whole body would be free of the mud. She heard the wind picking up at the mist and knew the Great Spirit was coming to cleanse her. She felt the pulsating mist spraying her chest and back. It was not spraying the clean parts of her body, and she was so thankful because that would have really hurt. Kaila began her part of the cleansing.

"I feel ugly.

"I feel bad.

"I feel great shame.

"I feel stupid.

"I feel this awful mud is my fault.

"I feel so lost and all alone."

With that last thought Kaila started crying. She was beginning to feel much pain and it hurt her heart. However, Kaila wanted freedom from the mud, so she continued right through her tears.

"I feel unlovable.

"I feel crazy.

"I feel broken!"

The pulsating mist grew stronger. She started feeling the pain of the cleansing mist coming closer and closer to her skin and heart. She began to sob and shake. She wished it would stop, but she wanted to be cleaner. And just as she felt she could stand no more, the cleansing mist moved away and settled in front of the rocks again.

Kaila was worn out by the time this cleansing was through, and Juta, who had been right beside her the whole time, gently urged her to lie down and rest. It had taken a lot of energy out of her not to scream stop and to hold on until the Great Spirit was through. Kaila looked up into Juta's face for reassurance. She fell fast asleep knowing she was safe with Juta nearby.

Kaila slept the rest of that day and the entire night, stirring very little. Long before midday, she opened her eyes and looked up into Juta's face. Juta's eyes were closed, and Kaila knew again that Juta was in his safe place. She lay there in silence, grateful she had found Juta. Finally, Juta opened his eyes, looked at Kaila, and touched her on her cheek. Kaila laughed.

"Juta, how long have I been asleep?"

"You have been asleep for as long as you needed, Kaila."

"Thank you for staying near, Juta."

Kaila sat up heavily. She thought, "Something is wrong. I still have mud on me from my waist down. I don't remember screaming stop to the Great Spirit, and they said I would be the one to choose when I had had enough. I wonder what happened. Did the

Great Spirit get tired and stop? Or maybe they ran out of their cleansing mist? After all, I had lots of layers of old dried mud on me. Juta will know."

"Juta," she asked, "what happened? I still have mud on me from my waist down. How can that be? I thought I'd be *all* free!"

Juta knew this would be hard for Kaila to accept, and while she had slept Juta and the Great Spirit had decided it would be best for Mama Spirit to answer any questions and lead the final cleansing.

"Everything is as it should be, Kaila. You have one final cleansing to go. Mama Spirit will be very happy and honored to explain this to you."

"What could this other cleansing be? If *I* don't know, how could the Great Spirit know? Why am I so afraid to ask Mama Spirit what comes next?"

Kaila heard the mean voice from within speaking to her. It was definitely losing its power because she could hardly hear it.

"Kaila, take what cleansing you have gotten and get out of here. You have a chance to remain one with your mud family for you still have some mud on you. If you continue you will no longer be a part of your mud family. I'm telling you, Kaila, this will bring great sadness and pain to your mud family. Who gave you the right to get better than them? They need you,

Kaila. You are being selfish. Go, go now and every-thing will be OK. You will not make it through this next cleansing, Kaila, you will die!"

"Stop, stop!" she screamed. "You are lying. I will not die and this will not hurt my mud family. My cleansing is going to help them. I will never listen to you and your lies again. You have no more power over me."

Kaila jumped up and ran over in front of the mist.

"Mama Spirit, Mama Spirit," Kaila cried, "please tell me what cleansing I have left. I don't understand why I'm still covered with mud from my waist down."

"Kaila, my child," Mama Spirit began, "has anyone touched you where you would not want to be touched?"

"Oh, no, I can't talk about that," Kaila thought. "That mean voice was right, I will die if I talk about it. It makes me feel ashamed and embarrassed. It's just too painful. How come Mama Spirit knows about it? Who told her?"

"Kaila, I know you feel frightened and ashamed about what happened to you. However, healing can only come when you allow those memories to surface. As you bring them out into the light your final cleansing can begin."

"You mean it will be all gone then?"

"Yes, Kaila, the rest of your mud will be all gone."

"Will I have to tell who did what and when?"

"No, my child, that won't be necessary. I already know."

"Well, if you already know, Mama Spirit, why do I have to remember all those painful times?"

"Only you have the power to break the secret of hidden pain in this area. I can cleanse you of the mud, but not without your help. If you choose not to go through this final cleansing, you will be loved by us anyway. Our love does not depend on the amount of cleansing you are brave enough to go through. Our love is always yours because we choose to freely give it to you. This is a hard decision for you to make. You are a delight to us, Kaila, and it is fine for you to go home now if you need time to think about this. If for some reason you decide not to go through this last cleansing, that is OK. You can come back to see us anytime."

Kaila was feeling so stuck. She loved the part of her body that was now free and without the mud. She sure would like to have the rest of her body free. She wondered if she did have the courage to break this family secret. "Maybe Juta can help," she thought.

Kaila turned around and there was Juta. She walked over to him with her eyes down and said, "Juta, do you think I can be brave enough to get the rest of my mud off?"

"Yes, Kaila, I do. You have great inner strength, and I promise to stay close by and pray for you the whole time."

"Juta, I'm not sure you will like me after I tell you and Mama Spirit this secret."

Juta instantly began to laugh. His laughter was filled with joy and it started Kaila laughing. Once she began to laugh Papa Spirit joined in and the whole falls shook with laughter. As a matter of fact, Mama Spirit let go of her composure and laughed the hardest. Her laughter sounded like Reeny's laugh to Kaila. It seemed like they would laugh forever, but thank goodness they all finally stopped. Papa Spirit had the hardest time getting his composure, so once again Mama Spirit had to give him a gentle, loving nudge. Soon all was quiet.

"Juta, what was that all about?" asked Kaila.

"Kaila, both the Great Spirit and I have always known your secrets. We will always love you, no matter what kind of secrets you have."

Kaila wrapped her arms around Juta's waist and cried, "Juta, let's get started and get this over with. I'm glad you are here with me."

"We are ready, Mama Spirit, to finish Kaila's final cleansing," said Juta.

"Kaila," said Mama Spirit, "this cleansing will be

different. To begin with, allow yourself to remember one by one each memory you have of this painful abuse. Also, Papa Spirit and I will not change into a pulsating mist. Instead, we have prepared a pool for you which has special water that is only waist deep. Just slowly enter the water until it covers your remaining mud. Papa Spirit and I will enter this special water and gently swirl it around you like it swirled around your ankles when you first entered the Mystical River."

"Oh, Mama Spirit, I'm afraid to go into water that is so deep because I can't swim. I'm scared I'll drown."

"I know you are afraid, Kaila, but you can trust Papa Spirit and me, we will not let that happen. This will be a painful and difficult cleansing. Learning to trust is an important part of getting your mud off. You have trusted Juta, Papa Spirit, and me several times. When this cleansing is over you will experience the joy of knowing for certain that there are those who are worthy of your trust."

Kaila liked the way that sounded. She would somehow, through this final cleansing, learn the joy of trusting others who are safe.

"Mama Spirit, is it OK if I holler when it starts to hurt bad? I am never allowed to holler at home when anything or anyone hurts me. I think hollering would help, don't you?"

The Mud People

❖

"You may holler as loud as you like, Kaila. The roar of the falls is pretty loud. I wonder if you can holler louder than that."

Mama Spirit was so kind to let Kaila know it was absolutely OK to yell when in pain. She gave Kaila a little suggestion to see if she could out-holler the roar of the falls because she knew, as gentle as Papa Spirit and she would be in removing this final mud, Kaila had much pain to face.

"Whenever you are ready, Kaila, just start walking into the pool of water that is right in front of you."

Kaila turned to face Juta, who was standing behind her, for a reassuring hug.

"I'll be right here, Kaila, only a few feet from you. You can trust me to help you just like I did on the journey down the Mystical River."

Kaila thought about that and how Juta had come to her rescue every time she needed help. She turned from him, feeling confident that he would not fail her now.

Kaila entered the pool of water and slowly walked until she was waist deep. She felt her body trembling, but she knew she was in safe hands.

When Kaila stopped walking Mama Spirit said, "Begin to let the memories surface from within you, Kaila. As you do that, Papa Spirit and I will enter the water and start our final cleansing. You are almost mud free!"

The cleansing of this mud was very painful, and with the surfacing of the memories, Kaila felt a scream that was welling up from deep inside her. And when she could hold it back no longer she let out an agonizing primal scream. It broke through the falls and the entire Mystical River was filled with its sound. The birds stopped their whistling. The wild-flowers that lined the Mystical River on both sides bent over and fell into the river in an effort to connect with the hurting child. All the mud people who were peeking out through the reeds knelt down and prayed for her. And the little mud children cried with her. Kaila's scream went out into the darkness of the forest and her mud family heard it. They had no idea it was their mud Kaila screaming with pain.

Everyone and everything was silent both in and around the Mystical River and the dark forest. It appeared the whole of creation was *one* with this very brave mud child who was getting the very last of her mud cleansed.

When at last the memories had stopped, Juta entered the pool of water to help bring Kaila out to safety. The Great Spirit, both Mama and Papa, had openly wept during this last and final cleansing.

The Mud People

↓

Juta guided Kaila to lie down on a bed of soft feathers he had prepared for her. Just before Kaila fell into a sound sleep she felt someone kiss the tears from her cheeks. It was then she became aware, if only for an instant, of Juta beside her. She briefly looked up at Juta's tear-filled eyes and then closed her eyes and went to sleep. And while she slept she dreamt the mud was gone. Little did she know it was no dream, as she slept quietly, clean and free for the first time in her life.

CHAPTER 6

Juta Explains Recovery

When Kaila opened her eyes she felt disoriented and still a little tired. Her throat was sore and she wondered if she had out-hollered the falls. Juta spoke softly,

"Good morning, Kaila, how are you feeling?"

"I feel a little stiff and sore and . . ."

Juta started laughing, which stopped Kaila from speaking, and she sat up to ask what was so funny. For some reason, unknown to her, Kaila seemed to have a lighthearted effect on Juta and the Great Spirit at times. It was then, as she moved to sit up, she realized her body was not stiff or sore.

"OH, OH, OH, I AM FREE!"

Kaila jumped up, screaming, "Juta, Juta, it's gone. All my mud is gone!"

"Yes," said Juta, laughing, "all your mud and muddy condition are gone!"

Kaila was jumping around dancing, laughing, and clapping her hands. She flopped back down on the ground and began to wiggle all her toes, one at a time.

"Look at my toes, Juta, even they are cute!"

Well, that did it! Juta couldn't contain his joy and love for Kaila any longer. He let out his wonderful, joyous laughter. Of course, right behind him, if not actually first, came Papa Spirit. He was well into celebrating the moment! Mama Spirit joined in, too. Kaila was laughing, dancing, and crying all at the same time.

Their laughter soared through the roar of the falls and rang out over the Mystical River. The birds were the first to hear it and join in with their whistling. The wildflowers came back up out of the Mystical River and opened their petals in a spray of magnificent color. The mud people clapped and cheered. The little mud children managed even in their muddy condition to move around and join the freedom dance with Kaila. The laughter drifted back into the dark forest, but Kaila's mud family was unable to hear it. Their house was filled with great sorrow.

Once again, all of creation was one in celebrating the faith, courage, strength, and love of a small free child.

At last Kaila could dance and laugh no more. Juta and Mama Spirit stopped, but Papa Spirit was enjoying it too much to stop yet. Again Mama Spirit gave Papa Spirit a gentle, loving, nudge and he managed to get himself under control.

"Kaila," spoke Mama Spirit, "will you please come here and stand right in front of us?"

Kaila did what was asked of her.

"Kaila, Papa Spirit and I will be leaving here soon to go to another place of cleansing."

"Oh," said Kaila, breathless, "you mean there are other Mystical Rivers in other places, and Great Falls, too?"

"Yes, child," answered Papa Spirit, "there are areas where Mama Spirit and I travel that are also places of cleansing and healing. There are several throughout the world. We go where the brave mud people like yourself are, those who have taken their journey and are ready to be set free."

"But before we leave, Kaila," said Mama Spirit, "we

have three questions to ask you. The first is what do you now think about yourself?"

Kaila looked up into the mist, where she knew they were watching her, and said, "I think I am a very beautiful little girl!

"I think I have much goodness within me!

"I think I am very bright, with lots of wonderful things to learn!

"I think whatever was wrong with me was cleansed away and I am just fine.

"I think I am worthy of love, safety, and closeness because you have all given so much of that to me.

"And I think now that the mud on me was not my fault."

Kaila became very quiet. She was surprised at how much her thinking had changed. She thought, "How wonderful to think such good thoughts about yourself."

Papa Spirit spoke next.

"Kaila, how do you now feel about yourself?"

"I feel beautiful!

"I feel good!

"I feel whole!

"I feel bright!

"I feel free!

"I feel found and surrounded with Spirit Presence!

The Mud People

"I feel so loved!

"I feel healed!"

"I'm glad there's nothing left to feel," thought Kaila. "I think I'd burst!"

"Kaila, you are truly healed and have with you now your true self," said Mama Spirit. "Papa Spirit and I have a gift for you."

"A gift for me? But you already gave me the very best gift of all. You gave me my freedom and got my mud off."

"No, child, you gave those gifts to yourself. It was you who chose every step of the way, to be free and without mud. Papa Spirit and I have the ability to remove the mud. But it was only after you brought all your pain, abuse, and shame out into the light that we could help you. So you see, you gave those gifts to yourself. Without your choice and desire to be free, Papa Spirit and I could spray and spray, but we would be unable to remove your mud."

Kaila was somewhat confused by all this, but she knew Juta could help her understand what it all meant.

"Our final question, Kaila, has to do with us giving you our gift," said Papa Spirit. "Tell us child, what does your name, Kaila, mean?"

"It means 'filled with fright.'"

"Do you still think and feel you are filled with fright?"

"Oh, no, Papa Spirit. I think I am a child filled with much love and peace now."

"Our gift to you, Kaila, is a new name," explained Mama Spirit. "Although it will still sound the same, it is not. We have changed the first letter in your name from 'K' to 'C.' The first letter in any name is the most important and carries the meaning. Caila will now mean 'filled with wonderment and light.' Do you like that, Kaila?"

Kaila whooped with delight and excitement, and tears began flowing down her clean face.

"Yes, oh yes, I love my new name. Please, Papa and Mama Spirit, when can I have it?"

"Is now too soon?" asked Mama Spirit.

"Oh, no," cried Kaila, "it could not be soon enough!"

"Fine, child, just kneel down where you are and you will be given our gift."

Kaila knelt down before the brilliant mist. Her heart was pounding so fast in her chest she could hardly breathe. She felt a gentle hand on her head and she knew it was Juta's. Next, the wind picked up and the mist began to move toward her. "Oh, I hope this won't be like the cleansing mist," she thought. It was then she felt the most wonderful warm, soothing water being poured over her body. She heard both Papa and Mama Spirit say together, "Kaila, we baptize you in this healing water and call you by your name, which shall be from this day forward, Caila, which means 'filled with wonderment and light.'"

Caila knelt very still for she knew she was in a holy, mystical moment. She heard the wind pick up and it got stronger. She then heard "Goodbye, for now, Caila," and the mighty wind went straight up and out of the Mystical River.

Caila stayed where she was for quite a while. She felt warm and loved and she now had a new name. Caila! She sat down and opened her eyes and saw Juta. He was nearby resting again in his safe place. Just as she was about to call him he opened his eyes.

"The Great Spirit is gone, isn't it?"

"Yes, Caila, the Great Spirit was needed somewhere else."

"Will I ever see or hear the Great Spirit again, Juta?"

"The Great Spirit is always with you, Caila. It lives in your very spirit, so you are never separated from it."

"But, Juta, I can't see or hear the Great Spirit as I have over the past few days. It's all different."

"You have no need right now to see or hear the

Great Spirit, so you won't. If you needed Mama or Papa Spirit you would definitely hear them. It's up to the Great Spirit, Caila, how and when to make their presence known. You may not see a mist, but you will always hear them within you. You will probably hear the Great Spirit much more over your lifetime than you will see them. The important thing to remember is that they are closer to you than the very breath you breathe. Remember, you are never, not even for a moment, separated from them or their love."

"Is it OK, Juta, if I don't understand all of this right now? It's good to know that I am never separated from the Great Spirit and their love for me. That is enough for me now. I can trust and believe you because I know you don't lie, right Juta?"

"That's right, Caila, and it is just fine for you to understand and take in whatever you can. You will grow in understanding and wisdom as you yourself grow. You understand the most important part."

Caila sat quietly for what seemed like hours. She had a big question to ask Juta, but she felt timid. She would have thought that by now she could freely ask Juta anything.

Juta knew exactly what Caila's question was before she asked it. He knew this particular question had bothered the child for a long time. He was glad she

had enough energy left to ask her question now. He wanted to help her understand all about recovery before she left to return home.

"Juta?"

"Yes, Caila."

"Please, can you tell me why innocent children have to get covered with mud? Why do even bigger people sometimes have to get a mud covering? Why, Juta, why do people hurt little children if we are not bad and it is not our fault? Please try to help me understand this."

Caila's eyes were filled with sorrow and her body felt the pain of grief. Quickly her face was wet with tears.

"Caila, would you like to climb into my lap so I can hold you and try my best to explain all this?"

Caila quickly scampered into Juta's arms. He held her close and rocked her for a while. He then began to answer her most important question.

"Caila, it was never meant that anyone should ever be covered with mud. At the very beginning, no one was. But one day some people stopped believing in goodness and truth and wanted to start their own way of thinking and feeling about things. So they separated themselves from the presence of the Great Spirit."

Caila was listening very intently as Juta talked and rocked her in his arms.

"When people are separated from the truth of the Great Spirit, they make up their own form of truth. But it is a false truth based on lies. Those people who are separated from the truth begin by first lying to themselves and then to their children. Their children don't know it is a false truth, so they in turn pass it on to their children and their families. The more it gets passed down, the bigger the lies become. A false self is then created within each who believes the lies. Soon the lies become secrets, and the secrets must be kept at all costs to preserve the false truth. Then the abuse begins. Parents hurt their little children and scare them into keeping the secrets because they believe that is what they are supposed to do. So on and on it goes. The secrets are passed down from one generation to another, and with each passing the abuse and cruelty gets worse and worse and keeping the secrets becomes the most important thing. Are you able to follow me so far, Caila, or is this too much for you to understand?"

"I think I understand. But why can't the Great Spirit stop all the lies and abuse before it hurts us, Juta?"

"The Great Spirit has given each of us a very

blessed and sacred birthright. Part of this birthright is a gift of choice. It is a most wonderful gift, Caila. The Great Spirit gave up control of us loving them in return in order for us to be free to choose to love them. They very much want our love, just like you want your mud family to love you. But the Great Spirit lets us choose to love them or not."

"Well, Juta, what does the Great Spirit do then? I mean what if no one wanted to love them?"

"That would truly be awful, Caila. What the Great Spirit does is wait. They wait until there is born into a certain ancestry, or family, a mud child who is brave enough and desires enough to find the real truth. It is a child who has learned at a very young age that there is a tiny spirit of truth inside itself. You see, when a child is first born, it is born in the real truth. And if it learns to listen to this voice within, it will begin to know the real truth."

"What happens, Juta, if the child does hear the real truth? How does that child end up with a mud covering?"

"A child is completely dependent on its family. Although it may know the real truth, even just a little bit, if the child's family is from the false ancestry, then the child is being taught the false truth. After a while, the child might find it easier and less confusing to just know one truth and so picks up the one everyone else around it is living."

"Then what happens, Juta? How does the real truth ever get out?"

"There are some little children, like yourself, who choose to hold on to the real truth, in spite of great struggle, fear, ridicule, and much abuse. You see, Caila, you refused to believe that your birthright was one of abuse, shame, cruelty, and loneliness. You heard the small inner voice of truth within you, telling you there was more to life than what had happened to you in the shadows of the dark forest. You wanted to believe, and you suffered greatly to hold on to that. Do you remember the day you became brave enough, Caila, to venture out from the sunless forest?"

"Yes, Juta, I do remember that day. How could I ever forget? That was the day I met you!"

"Yes, Caila, that is right. That was a very special day. I had been waiting for you at the river's edge, among the reeds, from the day your existence began. I waited and waited and hoped and prayed that one day you would be brave enough to see for yourself what lay beyond the dark forest. I, too, will remember that day forever."

Caila took a minute before going on and gave Juta a hug.

The Mud People

❧

"So then what happens, Juta?"

"Well, what happens is exactly what happened. You slowly began to trust the truth I was sharing and teaching you, and you chose to take your journey to find your real self. You went down the Mystical River in spite of your fears, muddy condition, pain, separation from your family, and uncertainty. When you or anyone goes through the process of cleansing, a wonderful mystical miracle happens!"

"Oh, what is it, Juta? Tell me, tell me!"

Caila knelt on Juta's knees and put her hands on his face so she could look deep into his serene eyes and see and hear all about this miracle.

"When you are cleansed, Caila, your ancestry of lies is broken! You can then begin to pass down the wonderful ancestry of recovery. So from generation to generation, from family to family, the real truth is passed down. Slowly but surely, as more are cleansed, and more ancestries of recovery are started, the whole universe can one day be mud free!"

"Oh, Juta, am I really a part of the ancestry of recovery and truth?"

"Yes, Caila, you are a very special part."

With that she sat quietly near Juta trying to think about and feel everything he had just said. She felt so special. She knew she had just had a mystical moment of truth with Juta. She wanted it to last forever.

"Juta, it's time now for me to go home to my mud family. I can't wait until they see me without my mud. They won't recognize me, I bet! They will follow me right to the river's edge to see you. Just think, Juta, my whole family will be cleansed of their mud, and, Juta, we will all smell so nice and be children of the recovery ancestry!"

"Caila," cautioned Juta softly, "your mud family may not even see that you are mud free."

"What? How can that be, Juta? I do look different without my mud, don't I?"

"Yes, child, you look very different and very beautiful. However, not everyone will be able to see that. Some of your mud family might, perhaps, right away. It may take time for some others, and some may never notice you are without mud."

"Why, Juta, why?"

"Because some of your mud family, relatives, friends, and neighbors are covered with layers of denial mud. It was the only way for them to survive all the trauma and pain that happened to them. Some are covered with layers of blame and fault mud. These two layers make it very hard for them to hear their true voice from within. Caila, when a mud person who is covered with either blame, fault, or denial layers decides to take the cleansing journey, there is much rejoicing among the recovery people. We must wait the longest for those mud people to come to the river. Their cleansing takes longer because those layers are much thicker."

Caila grew very quiet as she tried to figure out how these different layers of mud might keep her mud family from seeing she was now clean. She wanted them to notice so they could go to Juta for help also.

"Juta, why do these layers of mud get in the way of my mud family and friends seeing I am without my mud? I thought you told me that my journey down the Mystical River and cleansing would help all of them."

"That is right, Caila. Your cleansing can be a very big help to all of them, *if* they choose to see your new truth. Recovery is about many things, and it starts with first acknowledging that you have been abused. It is hard for most people to arrive at this first step of truth finding. You see, Caila, to admit you have been abused and taught a false truth about yourself is very painful. You must come to accept the fact that you have been robbed of your birthright, and for most abused people it was taken at an early age. Knowing this causes one to feel much rage, anger, pain, and grief. It takes courage for one to face all of this."

"It is hard, Juta, to face that your mud family, especially your mom and dad, are not able to give you what you need to help you know the real truth about yourself. It's hard because little children trust their parents and family."

"The next part is even harder for most people to face!" said Juta.

"Oh, you mean there is more? What could that be?"

"The next part is to face the truth about yourself. You are a young child now, Caila, so for the most part you have been on the receiving end of the abuse. However, if you had decided not to take your journey and accepted your muddy condition, you would have developed layers of denial mud yourself. Then as you continued growing older you would have begun to blame others for your unhappiness and false belief system about yourself. When you blame others for the way you feel about yourself and do nothing to change that, then you begin to feel that whatever you do to others is not your fault."

"But, Juta, it's not my fault! If I don't know any better, how can it be my fault if I grow up and treat others the same way I was treated? After all, that is what I was taught."

The Mud People

❧

"Caila, do you remember what I said to you a short while ago about everyone being born in truth and without mud?"

"Yes, I do."

"One never loses that spark of truth. It does get covered over with layers of false truth, but anyone at any time can discover this spark of truth within. One has only to want to change and then work hard to bring it about. Your journey down the Mystical River and getting your mud removed was hard for you, wasn't it?"

"It sure was, Juta. There were times when I didn't think I had enough courage or strength to make it through all of the cleansings. The last one was the very worst for me."

"Each time, though, Caila, you made a decision to keep going, 'no matter what.' That's how you said it if I remember correctly!"

Caila laughed hearing Juta repeat her words. "Juta remembers everything!" thought Caila.

"So you see, no matter what happens to us we always have a choice to make about the way we choose to treat others. If people spend their lives blaming others for the way they have been treated, then only the false truth can be passed on. The abuse one receives as a child is *never* the child's fault. However, when a child grows up, it is then responsible for the truth it passes on. It is a choice, Caila, and no one can take responsibility for what is passed on except the person who passes it on. Can you understand what I am trying to teach you?"

"Yes, I think I do. Is it ever too late to find the real truth within, Juta?"

"No. As soon as a person decides to find the truth this person is already beginning to receive it. And the wonderful thing about finding the truth is that the person can then start to pass on the real truth and enter into the recovery journey. If people decide never to seek the truth it is very sad because their lives are then lived without ever finding their birthright. It cannot be discovered until the mud is removed and they have found their true self."

"Will I discover my true birthright now?"

"Yes, Caila, you have already begun. As you grow in recovery you will learn more and more, one day at a time, what your birthright is and all the gifts and special abilities you have been born with. You and I and all who have gone through their cleansing journey can pray and hope that those who are still covered with mud will be able to see us, the mud free, walking among them, helping them find their truth."

The Mud People

✦

"Juta, I will try my best to help my mud family know their truth."

"I know you will because I know you love them. One last thing, though. Remember, everyone must have the freedom of choice, especially when it comes to recovery. You or I or the Great Spirit cannot force recovery on anyone. That would be going against the person's birthright of choice. Just continue to love your mud family as always. In time, I'm quite sure, there will be some who will choose to take their journey down the Mystical River. Do you understand this, Caila?"

"You are telling me, Juta, that I must learn to wait like you and the Great Spirit. I must wait 'for as long as it takes' for the ones I love and care about to choose recovery. Is that right?"

"That's right, Caila. You are very bright and your family and friends can learn much from you, if they so choose."

"I guess this is goodbye, then, Juta."

And with that Caila began to cry because she just hated leaving her truest, safest friend.

Juta held the little child close and said, "Caila, I, like the Great Spirit, will always be with you. I'm only a heartbeat away. You will always know where to find me. I promise when you come back to the river, I will be waiting for you at your special place. You and I both have a great job to do. Our cleansing light can shine for others to see the way of recovery. And, Caila, it happens most by just being who you were meant to be, which is a beautiful child of the universe! Don't get caught up in doing. The truth is most known and understood through *being*."

"That's a little hard for me to understand, Juta. Is that one of those ideas that I will grow to understand?"

"Yes, Caila, it is another one of those truths you will in time grow to understand."

Juta took Caila by the hand. Together they walked out from under the falls into the sunlight. They were standing right in the Mystical River where Caila had first stepped. It seemed like a lifetime ago. The river was swirling around her ankles and Caila began to laugh. It was still ankle deep!

Caila threw her arms around Juta's waist and hugged him tight. She tried hard not to cry, but she could not hold back the tears. She was crying with both joy and sorrow. She loved Juta, and his help and friendship had brought her to her place of wonderment and light.

"It is so hard to let go of Juta," Caila thought. "But I know I can trust that he will be with me and I can come back and see him anytime. I know it is hard for Juta, too, because I feel his tears on my hair."

Caila squeezed Juta one last time and then let go and started running through the shadows of the dark forest toward her home. Somehow the forest didn't seem dark or scary anymore. She stopped one last time to turn and look at Juta. He was sitting by the river's edge in his safe place.

"I love you, Juta," Caila hollered, and off she ran, toward her home.

CHAPTER 7

A Homecoming

As Caila approached her house she noticed there were several mud relatives, neighbors, and friends on her front porch. She saw something dark hanging on the front door of her house. She noticed that everyone seemed very sad, and this frightened her. She quickly ran up the front steps and into the house.

She wondered why everyone was acting so strange. Hardly anyone noticed her, and those who did, did not seem to notice she was without her mud. "Juta was right, as always," thought Caila. "Some will not notice my clean condition." She quietly entered the living room to find her mud family seated there. Quickly she looked around to see if everyone was present. Not seeing Reeny, she walked over to her mud mother and said, "Mud mother, where is Reeny?"

Her mud mother looked at her very strangely. Caila thought perhaps it might be because she was noticing Caila had no mud! She sat there staring at her with a blank look on her face. Caila asked her again.

"Mud mother, where is Reeny?"

Suddenly her mud mother screamed at her.

"You stupid, ugly, mud child, what are you saying? You know as well as the rest of us that Reeny is dead!"

"Oh no," screamed Caila, "no, that can't be."

She ran out of the room and up the stairs to Reeny's bedroom. All the way she was screaming, "Reeny, Reeny, where are you? It's me, Caila! I'm home, and I'll take good care of you again. Reeny, Reeny, look, here I am!"

She pushed open Reeny's bedroom door, only to find the bed empty and stripped. She felt cold with terror and disbelief.

"No, no, no," she screamed. "It's a trick. I know it. Reeny, please come out and see me. Please, it's me,

The Mud People

⋎

Caila. Are you mad at me for being away? Is that why you are hiding?"

Reeny did not come out from anywhere, so Caila ran as fast as she could back downstairs and into the living room and right over to her mud father.

"Mud father, please, you will tell me, won't you, where is Reeny hiding?"

Her mud father turned to look at her but would not answer. He was not seeing her. He was off somewhere else, it seemed. Caila began to holler in pain because it hurt so bad. Her mud mother got up from her chair and slapped her hard on the face. It really hurt Caila because the mud coverings were gone. Her mud mother screamed at her again. "You stupid, ugly, mud child, how dare you feel like that in front of us. Are you crazy? Have you lost your mud manners? You know there is no feeling allowed in this house. Go outside before I lose my temper and give you the beating you deserve!"

Caila quickly ran outside and sat at the bottom of the porch steps. She knew she had just heard three lies about herself. One, that she was stupid. Two, that she was ugly. And three, that she was muddy. Those lies could not hurt her now because she knew the truth about herself. The slap hurt, but she could handle that. She had to remember that her mud mother

113

didn't know her truth yet. To protect herself, Caila vowed not to show her feelings in front of her mother.

Caila lowered her head to her knees and began to sob.

"It's all my fault, it's all my fault. I should have never left Reeny's side. If I had stayed home she would still be alive."

Caila sobbed and sobbed until she thought her heart would break. She started to hear Mama Spirit's voice softly within her.

"Caila, remember, it is never about fault. It's not your fault Reeny has died. Reeny's mud body could hold no more mud. That is why she died. She wants you to live and be happy. She will still be with you in your spirit, for we are always connected in the spirit. Try to be at peace, child."

With that, Mama Spirit was gone.

"I don't want Reeny to be gone. I want to see and touch her and hear her wonderful laughter. I want to look into her eyes and feel her love for me. I want her to see me now without my awful mud and I want her to be free also."

Caila started sobbing all over again as she lowered her head back to her knees.

Caila sat there crying for a long time. At some

point, she felt a small body pushing up against hers. She yelled "Ouch" because this person's mud was rough against her skin and it hurt. Caila looked up to see her youngest sister, Geri Girl, sitting beside her. As their eyes met Geri Girl said, "Caila, no mud! Caila, no mud!"

Caila scooped her up into her arms. She was the only one who noticed she was without her mud. She squeezed her very tight, and she didn't even care if Geri Girl's mud hurt her skin. She was so happy to see Geri Girl again.

"Geri look like Caila! Geri look like Caila!" her young mud sister said.

"Yes, oh yes, Geri Girl can look like Caila! Tomorrow morning I will take you to a very special friend I met by the Mystical River. He will help you to get your mud off. Is this what you want?"

"Yes, Geri Girl look like Caila!"

With that, they were called in to supper, and afterward everyone little was put to bed.

That night Caila lay awake for a very long time, quietly crying for Reeny. She just knew her heart was broken. She hoped the next day, when she saw Juta, he would be able to help her with this awful pain. She cried herself to sleep.

Early the next morning, Caila helped Geri Girl get

dressed, and together they started for the river's edge. Just as they were coming out of the dark forest, Caila asked Geri Girl to stop and wait there for her. She needed to speak to Juta by herself first. Geri Girl sat down to wait.

Caila ran to her favorite spot by the river and there as promised, sitting on a big rock, was Juta.

"Juta, Juta," she screamed, "Reeny is dead!"

Juta scooped Caila up into his arms and held the sobbing child. He sat back down and slowly rocked Caila. Her little body was quaking with sobs, and he rocked her until she could stop sobbing enough to speak. Juta's tears were mingled with hers.

At last Caila was able to stop crying. She needed to ask Juta a question.

"Juta, why, why did Reeny have to die now? I just know she would have made the journey down the Mystical River to be cleansed."

"Caila, Reeny was a very caring and brave person, but she could never trust quite enough to leave the shadows of the dark forest. Her body was weakened by all the mud that covered her, and this caused her to get sick and finally die."

"But, Juta, she never got a chance to see me without my mud, and worst of all, she died in her muddy condition."

The Mud People

✦

"Caila, I have a surprise for you. Reeny did see you without your mud! You see, there is another way to get mud off. The quickest way is to do just as you did. You took those first courageous steps to leave the darkness of the forest and take the journey down the Mystical River. However, as we discussed before, not everyone is brave enough or desires enough to take such a journey. Remember, it's not right or wrong, it's not about blame or fault. It's just some are never able to do it. So whenever a mud person dies, their spirit is brought directly into the Mystical River, and as soon as it hits the water, it is cleansed and finds its true self. The spirit part is the easiest to cleanse after someone dies. So you see, Reeny may have died in her muddy condition, but she is free of it now, just like you."

"But, Juta, when did she see me without my mud?"

"Just as your final cleansing finished, do you remember what happened before you went into a deep sleep?"

"I think so, Juta. I remember you kissing the tears off my cheeks."

"Your tears were kissed off, Caila, but it was not I who kissed them away. It was Reeny!"

Caila jumped off Juta's lap, shedding tears of joy.

"Juta, you mean Reeny was there with me?"

"Yes, Caila, her spirit had entered the Mystical River just as your final cleansing was complete. Reeny's freed spirit came down and kissed you goodbye. She saw how beautiful you looked. She stayed for as long as she could, watching over you with me while you slept. She was summoned to start her new Mystical Journey just before you woke up."

"So, her mud is gone and she is safe now forever?"

"That's right, her mud and pain are gone forever and she is very safe."

"Juta, one last question. What does Reeny look like without her mud?"

"She is very beautiful, Caila. Her spirit glows with a sparkling luster and her laughter shakes the heavens."

"Gosh, she and Papa Spirit will have great fun laughing together.

"Oh, I almost forgot!" said Caila. "Please wait right here."

Caila ran quickly to get Geri Girl. She hoped her wait hadn't been too long. Geri Girl was still there.

"Come, Geri Girl, I have someone very special for you to meet."

Caila took Geri Girl by the hand and led her to Juta.

"Juta, this is my baby mud sister. Her name is . . ."

"Geri Girl," said Juta.

"Juta, Geri Girl wants to get her mud off, so I will take her down the Mystical River to the Great Spirit."

"No," said Juta, "you cannot take her down the Mystical River. Everyone must go by themselves."

"Juta, she is much too little to go by herself."

"Yes, she is, so I will take her."

"Oh, Juta, I know she will be safe. You are the best safe person ever!"

"Thank you, Caila," said Juta. "I will gladly take her and keep her safe."

Caila had a question. "Juta, do you think you could come to my house sometime and talk to my mud mother and mud father about this Mystical River and the journey?"

"I would be glad to come to your house, Caila. But I don't think your mud mother or mud father will be able to take their journey down the Mystical River. They have a whole lifetime of mud layers, many of which are the denial layers. I sense they will most likely get their mud removed like Reeny, in death."

"Juta, it makes me feel so sad, especially for my mud mother. She has the most mud coverings in our family."

"I know it hurts you, so to help, I will tell you a mystical truth."

"A mystical truth! What is it, Juta?"

"Even though you cannot take your parents' mud off, you can soften it by your great love and understanding for them. Do you remember when you first stepped into the Mystical River?"

"I sure do, Juta."

"The water was ankle deep. Even though it didn't remove your mud, it did soften it. That made your ankles feel better, didn't it?"

"Oh, yes, it really did help with the pain and discomfort just to have the mud softer."

"That's what you do for anyone you really love, Caila. Your cleansed heart now has the power to soften other peoples' muddy condition."

Caila loved hearing that.

Juta held out one of his hands to Geri Girl. Together they all walked to the river's edge. Caila noticed a new little boat waiting to take Juta and Geri Girl down the river. She stood and watched as Juta got in first and then lifted Geri Girl into the seat beside him. He put a life jacket on her. Caila loved the way Juta knew how to make little ones feel safe. As soon as Geri's life jacket was on, the flow of the Mystical River started the wooden boat moving. Caila watched till they were out of sight, waving goodbye the whole time.

The Mud People

When Caila could no longer see Juta and Geri Girl, she turned around and marveled at the beautiful wildflowers.

"Oh, wildflowers, I'm so thankful you grow here. May I pick some of you for my mud mother? Even though she may never be able to come out of the dark forest, I'd like to bring your sunshine to her."

Caila grew still and she heard her inner friend say it would be fine for her to carry back some wildflowers to her mud mother. She started to pick as many as she could hold. She thanked each one for its life and beauty.

And, although she never would have thought it possible, Caila was going home, and happy about it!

ACKNOWLEDGMENTS

I am deeply indebted to so many people who have not only supported me in bringing this book to publication but also supported my very life and journey. At the risk of unintentionally overlooking even one such person, I choose to simply say that if you know me and any of my life's story, know that you are one that I want to personally thank and send my love to. From my children, Michael, Sarah, and Amie, to my family of origin, to hundreds of friends around the country, to the therapists who have helped untangle my life, to the fellow sojourners I have had the privilege to meet in treatment programs and support groups, this one's for you. I will always be eternally grateful for your touch on my life.

I want to say a special thanks to Joyce Norman, who worked with me on editing the book and for sending it to Joann Davis.

Thank you to Joann Davis, then the Senior Editor at Warner Books, for believing in my story. Thank you also to Caryn Karmatz Rudy, who became my new editor and worked closely with me to bring about the finished edition.

This next acknowledgment is very special and it's to David Hendin, my agent, who has blessed my life with abundant kindness, has helped me through the process of negotiating my contract, has never tired in answering my many questions, and has always gotten back to me in a timely manner. Thanks, David. I look forward to your help on my second book.

Last, but by no means least, my gratitude goes to Juliana Hamilton Chase, the illustrator for the book. Juliana agreed to do the paintings for me before we knew there would be a publisher and contract. She took a risk in giving of her time and talents and I know she will be blessed in many different ways for her graciousness in helping me. The pictures in the

The Mud People

✦

book, as you have seen, add so much to the story itself and are invaluable to me. Thanks, Juliana. You are an artist in the purest sense of the word and a dear friend to me.

LANEY MACKENNA MARK